Also in the Animal Ark Pets Series

LUCY DANIELS
Foal
Frolics

Illustrated by Paul Howard

*Hodder
Children's
Books*

a division of Hodder Headline plc

Special thanks to Linda Chapman

Animal Ark is a trademark of Ben M. Baglio
Text copyright © 1999 Ben M. Baglio
Created by Ben M. Baglio, London W12 7QY
Illustrations copyright © 1999 Paul Howard
Cover illustration by Chris Chapman

First published in Great Britain in 1999
by Hodder Children's Books

ISBN 0 340 73593 7

Typeset by Avon Dataset Ltd, Bidford-on-Avon, Warks

Printed and bound in Great Britain by
The Guernsey Press Co. Ltd, Channel Isles

Hodder Children's Books
a division of Hodder Headline plc
338 Euston Road
London NW1 3BH

Contents

In memory of Sophie –
a very special dog and friend

1

Setting up camp

"Are we nearly there?" Mandy Hope asked eagerly, as her father turned the Land-rover up a bumpy lane. She was longing to get to the campsite to see what it was like.

"About two minutes away," Mrs Hope answered as she looked round, her green eyes twinkling.

Mandy glanced excitedly at James, who was sitting beside her on the back seat. James Hunter was her best friend. The Hopes had invited him and his dog, Blackie, to come camping with them for a week in South Wales. Mandy's grandparents were coming as well.

"Look out for the sea," Mr Hope said, as the Land-rover climbed further up the hill.

"I bet Blackie's going to love the sea," James said to Mandy.

Mandy stroked the black Labrador puppy, who was sitting behind the dog guard in the back. "I bet Blackie's going to love *everything* about camping," she said. She loved going on holiday with Blackie. It was almost like having a pet of her own. Her parents had a vet's practice called Animal Ark in the village of Welford, where they lived. They were too busy looking after other people's animals to let Mandy have any pets herself, though.

"Do you think there'll be any other animals at the campsite?" she asked.

Mr Hope chuckled. "I'm sure you'll find some. You normally do!"

The Land-rover reached the top of the hill. "The sea!" James shouted suddenly. "Look, Mandy!"

The sea was spread out in front of them, glittering in the late afternoon sun. Green fields and cliffs lay in front of it.

"Wow!" said Mandy. "It's beautiful."

White caravans and multicoloured tents were dotted over the fields to the left. There was a track to the right. A very smart sign beside it said PENDELLI GOLF COURSE in big, gold letters. Mr Hope took the left turn through a gateway. It had a plain black and white sign on it saying: PENDELLI HILLTOP CARAVANS AND CAMPING.

Mandy checked out of the back window to see if Gran and Grandad were still following them in their car. They were. Grandad waved.

Just before the caravans, they reached a stone cottage. Baskets filled with flowers hung from hooks by the door. A man of about Mr Hope's age came out to meet them. He was wearing shorts and had dark curly hair. Mr Hope wound down the window. "Adam Hope and family," he announced. "We've got a caravan and two tent sites booked."

"Pleased to meet you," said the man, smiling broadly. "I'm Alex Hughes. I own the site. Follow me and I'll show you to your caravan and camping space."

They drove slowly behind him. Mandy leaned forward. "Gran and Grandad know Mr Hughes, don't they, Mum?"

Mrs Hope nodded. "Yes, they're friends of his parents. The Hughes haven't been here long. I think Gran said this was their first season as owners."

They followed Mr Hughes to the edge of the campsite, where the field ended and the cliffs fell away to the sea. He stopped by a gleaming white caravan. There was plenty of space around it for two tents.

"We're right next to the beach!" Mandy said.

"Come on. Let's get Blackie out!" James suggested, as Mr Hope stopped the Land-rover.

They all jumped out. Gran and Grandad came over to see Alex Hughes. "How's Fiona? . . . And Sara? And how are you all settling in here?" Gran asked.

"Very well," replied Mr Hughes. "It's hard work, but wonderful."

Mandy and James left them chatting and hurried over to the fence at the edge of the cliff. A light breeze ruffled Mandy's short blonde hair as she breathed in deeply. "Mmm. I can smell the sea."

"When you sniff like that, you look like Blackie!" James laughed.

Hearing his name, Blackie looked up. But when he saw he wasn't wanted, he bounded away, sniffing the grass and wagging his thick black tail. At the bottom of the cliff was a golden sandy beach. People were walking along it, enjoying the afternoon sun.

"I wonder what's over there," Mandy

said, pointing to the dark-green hedge that ran down the field, marking the edge of the campsite. Near it was a tall clump of trees.

Just then, a small white ball came flying over the hedge. Blackie ran playfully towards it and picked it up.

"Quick, James! Get it off him. He might swallow it," said Mandy in alarm.

Luckily James had some dog treats in his pocket. "Blackie! Fetch!" he called, rustling the bag. Blackie came trotting over with the ball in his mouth. "Good dog," said James, pleased. "Leave." Blackie dropped the ball at his feet.

Mandy picked it up. "It's a golf ball."

They took it over to the adults, who were still talking. "Look what came over the fence," Mandy said, showing them the ball in her outstretched hand.

Alex Hughes rolled his eyes. "Another one," he said. "It's one of the problems with having a campsite right next to a golf course."

"Isn't it a bit dangerous?" asked Mrs Hope, tucking a strand of her long red hair behind her ear.

"Well, we try not to have caravans or tents any nearer than yours," said Mr Hughes. "And there haven't been any accidents. Besides, I don't really want to complain because the golf course does encourage people to camp here."

Grandad nodded. "*We're* certainly planning a round of golf for tomorrow morning."

Mr Hughes turned and smiled at Mandy and James. "My daughter Sara must be about your age. She's nine."

"The same as me," said Mandy. "James is eight," she added.

"There aren't any other children staying here at the moment, so she'll be very pleased to meet you," Mr Hughes said. "She loves making friends with all the guests."

James grinned at Mandy. "Just like you with all the animals that come into Animal Ark!"

"She'll probably come and find you tomorrow," Alex Hughes added. Then, saying goodbye, he went back to the cottage.

"Right," said Gran, rubbing her hands together briskly. "Let's unpack." They set about unloading the cars. While Mr and Mrs Hope got the tents out, Mandy and James helped Gran and Grandad carry things into the caravan.

"Isn't this lovely?" said Gran, looking

around the clean, cosy caravan. There was a seating area at one end with a table and chairs, a bed that folded out, and a small kitchen area.

"There's a sofa, a kitchen and a shower!" exclaimed James.

"And a sink for the washing-up!" said Grandad, a twinkle in his eyes.

Mrs Hope poked her head round the door. "Do you want to come and set up your tent?" she asked Mandy and James.

"Yes please!" they both said at once.

They raced outside. Mr Hope was unfolding their tent. "Now, where do you want it?" he asked. "It needs to be somewhere flat."

"Not too close to the golf course!" said James. "We don't want to get hit on the head."

"Over here," said Mandy, choosing a spot just far enough away from her mum and dad's tent, and quite near the group of trees. "This looks quite flat."

Mr Hope showed them how to put up

their tent. They laid out the groundsheet, put in the tent pegs, slid in the poles and fastened down the over-sheet.

"That will stop you getting wet if it rains," Mr Hope explained.

Mandy and James collected their sleeping bags and rucksacks from the Land-rover and ducked inside the tent. "It's brilliant," said Mandy, looking round the little space. "And it's all ours!"

They laid out their sleeping bags. "Have you got *your* torch?" James asked, getting out his own.

Mandy nodded. "And I've also got . . ." she rummaged in her bag and pulled out an enormous bag of crisps, two bars of chocolate and a bottle of cola, ". . . a midnight feast!"

"Wow!" said James. There was a sudden rustling noise. Blackie pushed his way through the tent flap and came nosing towards Mandy. "All right. Of course we'll share it with you, Blackie," said Mandy, putting her arm round him.

Blackie wagged his tail. He looked as if he thoroughly approved of the plan.

Then they heard Mrs Hope calling them and they came out from the tent. "Gran's heating up a pie for supper," she told them. "Why don't you take Blackie for a quick walk? I'm sure he could do with one after that long car journey."

"Yes. Let's go down to the beach," Mandy said.

They set off down the cliff path. The

tide was out, but Blackie soon found some rock pools to play in. He tried to drink the water but stopped almost immediately. He turned to look at Mandy and James, a puzzled look on his face.

"He doesn't understand that it's salty because it's seawater!" James grinned as Blackie spat out the water and raced off down the sands.

Mandy and James found another path leading up the cliff and decided to explore. There was a fence at the top, and on the other side of the fence was the golf course. The grass was so green and well-looked after that it almost looked like a carpet.

"I wonder what that man's doing," said James. He was watching a short, thin man peering at the grass around one of the holes nearest to them.

"He's probably the green-keeper," said Mandy, who had heard Gran and Grandad talk about golf before. "Green-keepers look after the grass."

"He looks a bit annoyed about something," said James.

Suddenly the man noticed them. "No entry!" he shouted, taking Mandy and James by surprise. "This is a golf course, not a playground! I'm not having children coming in here; climbing over the fences, messing up my greens and leaving litter."

Just then, Blackie came bounding up beside them. He wagged his tail and looked through the fence. The man's face darkened with rage. "And get that dog away from my golf course!"

"He's not doing any harm," Mandy protested.

The man glared. "What's that?" he demanded, striding angrily towards them. "Go on, clear off!"

James quickly pulled Mandy's arm. "Come on. Let's go."

They ran back down the path before the man could get any nearer. Blackie shot past them, almost tripping James over.

"What a nasty man!" Mandy burst out

as they reached the beach again.

"No entry!" said James, screwing up his face and imitating the green-keeper's bad-tempered voice. "Clear off!"

Mandy stopped feeling angry and started giggling. "Silly man! Come on, I'll race you back to the tent."

They charged along the beach, up the path and across the springy grass with Blackie at their heels. Mandy was just ahead. She reached the tent. "Beat you!" she gasped to James. Then she stopped dead.

James almost ran into the back of her.

"Look!" Mandy shrieked.

Their tent had been disturbed. One side had collapsed, two of the tent pegs had come out of the ground and the over-sheet had come loose.

James stared. "What's happened to it?"

Mandy ran over and ducked her head inside the opening. "James," she cried. The sleeping bags and rucksacks were still there, but their midnight feast had gone!

2

The Beast of Pendelli

Mr and Mrs Hope, Gran and Grandad all stared at the spoiled tent.

"But who could have done it?" Mandy said, clearly upset.

"It's a mystery," said Gran.

"I can't understand why we didn't see or hear anything," said a puzzled Mrs Hope.

"We've been in and out of *our* tent all the time. And you're *sure* nothing else has been taken?"

"No, everything's there," said Mandy. "My purse and my clothes."

"And all my things," said James.

"Maybe it was an animal," Mandy said.

Mrs Hope looked doubtful. "But what type? A squirrel or fox probably wouldn't have sniffed out the food as it was all sealed. Anyway, it wouldn't have uprooted the tent pegs and practically knocked the tent over."

"It could have been a really big dog," Mandy suggested.

"It would have had to be a Great Dane to do this sort of damage!" Mr Hope pointed out.

James's eyes widened. He had an idea. "Maybe it was one of those big wildcats you sometimes read about in the newspaper. The ones that people report seeing that are meant to be related to escaped panthers."

Mandy looked quickly at her mum and dad. "It could be, couldn't it?"

"The Beast of Pendelli!" said Mr Hope, with a chuckle.

Mrs Hope laughed, too. "Now you're being silly," she said to Mandy. "Even if there *are* such things as these cats, they certainly wouldn't be found on the edge of a campsite. They'd be somewhere with lots of space, well away from humans."

"So what did do the damage then?" Mandy asked her.

Mrs Hope shook her head.

"Like I said," Gran said, "it's a mystery . . . and best forgotten about." She put her arms round Mandy and James. "I'm sure I can find you some cakes and biscuits, so you can still have your midnight feast. Let's go and see what's in the caravan."

They followed Gran back to the caravan, but Mandy was very quiet. She was thinking hard. Something had knocked over their tent, that was certain. What if James *was* right and there was a wildcat living near-by? Or, if it wasn't a wildcat, maybe another type of animal that had escaped from somewhere. Excitement grew inside her. If there was a strange animal around, she was determined to find it.

It was such a warm night they were able to eat supper sitting on rugs on the grass, with their plates balanced on their knees. Blackie lay at James's feet, waiting hopefully for scraps of food.

"I'm looking forward to my first round of golf tomorrow morning," said Mr Hope. "Are you two going to caddie for us?"

Mandy and James nodded. Then James asked, "What does a caddie do?"

"Helps carry the clubs and fetch the balls when they go missing," Mandy's dad replied.

"I hope we don't meet that man," said Mandy, glancing at James.

"What man?" asked Mrs Hope.

Mandy and James explained about the bad-tempered green-keeper.

Grandad laughed. "Green-keepers can sometimes be a bit protective of their greens," he said. "After all, it's their job to keep them in as good a condition as possible. The smoother they are, the fairer and more enjoyable golf can be for everyone playing."

"But we wouldn't have done anything," said Mandy.

"We know you wouldn't, love," Gran said.

Mr Hope put down his plate and sighed.

happily. "That pie was delicious," he said. Blackie pricked up his ears and looked at him. "Yes, pie, Blackie," he said. "But it's all gone."

"Not all," said Mandy, looking at the plates. "Can we give Blackie the leftovers?" she asked.

Mrs Hope nodded. "But put them in his bowl. If you feed a dog at the table, it teaches him to beg. We don't want Blackie getting into bad habits."

Mandy and James took the plates into the caravan and scraped the rest of the supper into Blackie's bowl. In two seconds, the bowl was clean and Blackie was looking up for more. "Greedy thing!" said James. "That's it. It really is all gone now."

They went back outside and sat watching the sun go down. Mr and Mrs Hope kept everyone entertained by telling stories about different animals they had treated during their time as vets.

"We'll have to see what animals there

are around here tomorrow," said Mandy. "There must be some."

She looked towards the dark group of trees. Now it was getting dark, she wasn't sure she wanted a big wild animal to be lurking there . . . even if she *did* love all animals. Maybe it hadn't been a wildcat who disturbed their tent after all, Mandy thought, shivering a little.

"But what else could it have been?" asked James, as they got into their sleeping bags and zipped them up tightly. It was dark and they had to use their torches to see. Blackie didn't help: he had never spent the night in a tent before and couldn't decide where to sleep.

"I don't know," said Mandy. "Ow!" she squealed as Blackie trod on her tummy. Blackie lay down between the two sleeping bags. His warm body felt very comforting.

Mandy shone her torch on the roof of the tent. She could make circles and patterns. James tried too. They could hear the tiny scuttling of insects and spiders on the roof. "Have you got the midnight feast your gran gave us?" James asked.

Mandy nodded. "But we have to wait till midnight. Otherwise it's not a midnight feast."

James yawned. "Maybe we could just have a little sleep and wake up in a bit," he said.

Five minutes later, they were both fast asleep.

Mandy felt a warm tongue licking her face. She woke up and looked into Blackie's brown eyes. "Blackie!" she giggled. She wriggled out of her sleeping bag and poked her head out of the tent. Blackie bounded out across the grass. Mum and Dad were up and out of their tent already. Grandad was setting out a picnic table and chairs for breakfast. Mandy sniffed – the smell of frying eggs and bacon wafted from the open caravan door.

She quickly shook James. He groaned

and tried to go back to sleep. Mandy shook him again, and this time he opened his eyes. "It's morning," she said. "We slept through our midnight feast!"

James sat up and reached for his glasses sleepily.

"Gran's cooking breakfast," said Mandy. "Come on!" She pulled on some shorts, put a sweatshirt over her T-shirt and hurried out of the tent.

"Morning," said Dad. His blue eyes twinkled. "The Beast of Pendelli didn't get you in the night, then?"

Mandy grinned. Now it was morning, she felt much more relaxed about the idea of something living among the trees. In fact, she had decided that she and James would definitely go exploring later in the day to see what they could find.

"I like camping!" said James happily, as he sat munching a bacon sandwich and drinking a huge mug of tea.

"So does Blackie!" said Mandy, looking

at the dog, who was waiting hopefully for some food again.

"Time to clear up," said Mr Hope, finally getting to his feet.

"We'll help wash up," offered Mandy, picking up the plates.

"Why don't you two take Blackie for some exercise?" Mrs Hope suggested, when they had finished. "He won't be allowed on the golf course with us, so he'd better have a good long walk first."

"But where will we leave him when we go to the golf course?" asked James anxiously.

"He can stay in the caravan," said Gran. "I've brought something to keep him amused."

"What?" asked Mandy.

Gran winked. "A lovely, juicy marrow-bone."

Blackie loved his walk. He raced around on the sands and in the water, fetching a stick. By the time they got back, Blackie was tired out and quite ready to flop down on the floor of the caravan. Mr and Mrs Hope, Gran and Grandad had all changed into loose trousers and golf shoes. They settled Blackie on a blanket with a large bowl of water and his bone. Then they all set off for the golf club.

While Mandy and James were waiting for the adults to pay for their round of golf, they saw the green-keeper walking towards the clubhouse. He looked just as bad-tempered as the day before. "No entry!" muttered James to Mandy. She snorted with laughter, and the green-keeper looked sharply towards them. He frowned and, for a horrible moment, it looked as if he was going to come over, but then Grandad came out of the clubhouse and the green-keeper stomped off.

They started off round the golf course. At the second hole, Mr Hope hit the ball hard and it went flying off into the distance. It landed a long way ahead in the rough, the longer grass at the side of the course.

Mandy and James ran to find it.

"It was round here somewhere, wasn't it?" said James, starting to search through the grass.

"I think so," said Mandy turning in a full circle. There was no sign of the ball. "Maybe it went into those bushes."

But, as much as they hunted, they couldn't find it, so they went back to the adults. "We've looked everywhere," said Mandy. "The ball's lost."

Everyone broke off to have a quick look, but no one had any luck so Mr Hope took a shot with a new ball.

They walked on for a bit. Then Grandad hit a ball off the course. Again, Mandy and James searched and searched but they couldn't find it. "That one's gone as well now," said Mandy.

Once again, no one else could find it either. By the time this had happened at two more holes, everyone was feeling rather puzzled. "This is very strange," said Mrs Hope. "Balls don't just disappear into thin air. And you don't normally lose more than one ball on a round."

"We'll be running out of golf balls soon!" joked Gran.

They walked on. Mandy frowned and nudged James. "What if someone's stealing the balls?"

"But why would they do that?" said James.

Mandy shrugged. "To sell them," she suggested. "Golf balls are quite expensive. Let's try and find out."

They waited until another ball was hit off course. It flew into the air and over a hill. "We'll get it!" called Mandy. "Come on, James!"

Mandy and James raced after the ball. Reaching the top of the hill, they stopped dead. "Look!" shrieked Mandy.

They both stared.

A small brown–and–white foal was trotting through the long grass and bushes. Then it stopped. To Mandy and James's amazement, it reached down and gently picked up the ball between its lips!

"It's got the golf ball!" gasped James. "And it's taking it away."

They watched in silence as the foal turned and trotted back to the cover of the trees.

3

Mischief

Mandy and James stared at the foal. "What shall we do?" James said.

"Go after it!" Mandy exclaimed.

They ran down the hill. "We mustn't run when we get near," panted Mandy. "Or we may frighten it."

They reached the trees and slowed down.

"There it is!" whispered James. The foal was standing just inside the trees. It had a brown–and–white face and a fluffy brown mane and tail. Its tiny ears were pricked as it looked at them curiously.

Mandy picked a handful of grass and held it out. "Here, little foal," she murmured.

They stood still and waited. The foal stretched its head towards them and blew down its nostrils. It took the grass from Mandy's hand and stepped closer, pushing against her. Mandy stroked the foal's neck. "Isn't he lovely?" she said. "And he seems really tame."

James patted the foal as it tried to nibble his T-shirt.

"He looks well looked after," said Mandy, admiring the foal's bright eyes and shining coat.

James went to explore the area where the foal had been standing. "Look over here, Mandy," he called. Mandy and the foal followed him round the side of a bush. There, nestling in the long grass, was a pile of golf balls!

"He must have been collecting them," chuckled James. The foal nudged at the balls, picked one up in his mouth and then dropped it.

"I wonder who he belongs to?" said Mandy. "We can't leave him here, he might get on to the road. He must have escaped from a field somewhere." She looked around, wondering what to do.

The foal suddenly pricked up his ears and took a step forward. A girl came hurrying through the trees towards them. "Mischief!" she cried. "You naughty foal."

She stopped as she saw Mandy and James.

"Is he yours?" Mandy asked eagerly. "We found him on the golf course. We were just wondering what to do with him."

The girl smiled and came over. She had curly, dark hair and was carrying a small leather head-collar. "Yes, he's mine," she said, slipping the head-collar on the foal. "I live on the campsite just over there. My mum and dad run it. He lives there too,"

she said, patting the foal. "But he keeps escaping."

"You must be Sara," said Mandy. "We're camping on the site. We met your dad yesterday. I'm Mandy, and this is James."

"Oh, hi!" said Sara. "Dad told me about you." She patted the foal. "This is Mischief," she said.

"That's a good name for him." James laughed.

Sara grinned. "He's very naughty. He's always getting out from his paddock and knocking people's tents over. Sometimes he even steals their picnics. He moves really quietly so people hardly ever notice he's there."

Mandy gasped. "So it must have been Mischief who disturbed our tent and stole our midnight feast!"

Sara's hand flew to her mouth. "Oh no! When did he do that?"

"Last night," Mandy explained. "But don't worry. We don't mind, now that we know it was him. We love horses, don't we, James?"

James nodded. "We love all animals."

Just then, there was an angry shout from behind them. Mandy, James and Sara swung round. The grumpy green-keeper was striding towards them. "Oh no," said Sara, looking suddenly worried. "Here comes trouble."

The short, thin man stopped in front of them. "What is that animal doing on my golf course?" he shouted. Mischief snorted in alarm.

"I'm sorry, Mr Benson," said Sara. "He escaped again."

The little man looked as if his eyes were going to pop out of his head. "He mustn't be *allowed* to escape! He's making a mess of my greens, trampling all over them."

"I'll find out how he got out and stop him doing it again," said Sara. "I promise."

"You'd better keep that promise!" said Mr Benson, his mouth narrowing. "Or else I'll call the authorities and report him.

He should be kept tied up."

"But he'd hate that!" said Sara, in dismay.

"Well, make sure he stays in his paddock!" snapped Mr Benson. "You've been warned. Now, get him off my golf course!" Turning abruptly he stomped away.

Mandy and James looked anxiously at Sara. "Are you all right?" James asked her.

She shook her head. "I don't know what I'm going to do," she said. "If Mr Benson

complains to the authorities about Mischief, they'll make us keep him tethered. He'd hate it. He'd be sure to try and escape. And if he did, he might get tangled up in the rope and break a leg."

Mandy stared in alarm. She knew that if a pony broke its leg, it nearly always had to be put down. "You can't let that happen!" she exclaimed, looking at the tiny foal.

"But I don't know how he keeps escaping," Sara said.

Mandy's blue eyes flashed with determination. "Don't worry. We'll help you find out. Won't we, James?"

James nodded. "Of course."

"Really?" Sara looked at them hopefully. "Can you come back with me now?"

Mandy suddenly remembered that her mum and dad would probably be wondering where on earth she and James had got to. "We better go and find my parents first," she said rather guiltily. "But we'll catch up with you, if that's OK?"

"Of course," said Sara, suddenly looking much happier. "I'll meet you at the cottage. The stables are just behind."

Mandy and James ran back over the hill. They found Mr and Mrs Hope, Gran and Grandad near where they had left them. "Sorry!" panted Mandy.

"So what animal have you found this time?" asked Mandy's mum.

Mandy and James stared. How did she know about Mischief?

"There must be an animal," Mr Hope said, seeing their expressions. "Whenever you two go missing, it's normally because of a creature of some sort."

"We *did* find an animal," explained Mandy. "He's a foal called Mischief and he's in trouble!" She and James quickly explained about the foal and about the green-keeper's threat.

"We've got to try and help Sara stop Mischief escaping," said Mandy. "Otherwise he will have to be kept tied up."

Mrs Hope frowned with concern. "That won't make a happy foal, and it could also be quite dangerous," she said.

Mandy nodded. "That's why we've got to try and help. We said we'd meet Sara at the cottage." Her eyes pleaded with her mother. "Please, can we go there now?"

Mrs Hope nodded. "Of course. We'll come and find you when we finish here."

"Let's hope we won't lose any more golf balls, now the thief has been caught," Mr Hope said, picking up a golf club and giving it an experimental swing.

Mrs Hope chuckled. "That rather depends on how good your shots are!" She turned to Mandy and James. "Go on. Off you go."

"I hope you can help Sara," Gran said to them.

"We have to," Mandy replied, looking very determined. "Mischief's life might be in danger."

4

Lady

Mandy and James rang the doorbell of the cottage. Above the door, pretty hanging baskets filled with pink, purple and white flowers swayed gently in the breeze.

"Coming!" they heard Sara shout. She appeared from round the side of the house. "Hi!" she said. "The stables are round here. Come and have a look."

Mandy and James followed her. Just behind the back garden was a stable-block painted white, and a paddock with a sturdy wooden fence running all the way around it.

"There's Mischief!" said Mandy, seeing the little brown-and-white foal grazing beside a dapple-grey pony in the paddock.

"And that's Lady," said Sara, pointing at the grey pony. "She's his mother." She walked over to the gate. "Lady! Mischief! Come here."

The foal and his mother looked up and swivelled their ears. Sara rustled a sweet paper in her pocket. "Mints," she said, grinning at Mandy and James as Mischief and Lady started to walk over. "They love them. But they can't have too many because they're bad for their teeth." She handed Mandy and James some to give to the ponies.

"Lady's lovely," said Mandy, holding out her hand flat and offering the pony a mint.

Lady's lips tickled Mandy's palm as she gently took the sweet. She blew down her dark-grey nostrils at Mandy.

"That means she wants to be friends," said Sara.

Mandy grinned and stroked Lady's face. "I'd like to be her friend, too."

Mischief, who had obviously decided that his mother was getting too much attention, pushed past her and shoved his head into James's side. "Mischief's friends with anyone," Sara said with a laugh.

Mischief shoved at James harder. His head was just the right height to get James in the ribs. "Ow!" said James. He held out his last mint and Mischief gobbled it up.

"He's so greedy," said Sara, shaking her head, "*and* so clever. He keeps finding new ways to escape all the time. He got out by wriggling under the bottom rail of the fence to start with, so we fixed some mesh in the gap. Then he started getting out by squeezing between the top and bottom bars, so we put a strand of wire between

them. That seemed to stop him for a bit. Until yesterday, anyway."

"Maybe the wire or mesh has come loose," James suggested. "Have you checked it?"

Sara shook her head. They walked round the field looking at all the fences, but they couldn't see anywhere that Mischief could have escaped from. In the corner of the field down by the stables was a small gate that was swinging open on its hinges.

"Where does that go to?" James asked.

"Only to the muckheap," said Sara, shutting the gate and firmly drawing the bolt across. "I guess I must have left it open when I was mucking out the stables this morning."

"Could he get out that way?" Mandy asked.

Sara shook her head. "There's a fence all the way around the muckheap."

"What about the main field gate?" said James, looking round. "He has to be getting out *somewhere*."

"The main gate's got a bottom kick bolt," said Sara. "He couldn't open it." They went to investigate, and Mandy could see that Sara was right: The kick bolt was a heavy piece of metal on the stable side of the gate, and had to be pushed across to lock the gate at the bottom. Even if Mischief had found a way to undo the gate at the top, he would never be able to reach the kick bolt. The main gate was safe.

"You see, there's just no way he could have escaped," said Sara. "Someone must have let him out."

Mandy and James had to agree with her. It seemed almost impossible that Mischief could have got out of the paddock on his own.

"What can I do to make sure it doesn't happen again?" Sara asked them.

"If we hide, we could watch him to see how he is escaping," suggested James.

"Good idea," Sara said eagerly.

"We'll come round after lunch and help you then," said Mandy.

Just then, they heard the sound of voices. Adam and Emily Hope were coming down the path with a lady Mandy didn't recognise. She had short dark hair and lively brown eyes, and was wearing jeans and wellies. "Hi there!" they all called.

"Mum!" said Sara, hurrying through the gate towards the dark-haired lady.

"Mandy," called Mrs Hope, "this is Mrs Hughes." She turned to the lady. "Fiona, this is my daughter Mandy, and her friend James Hunter."

Sara's mother smiled at them. "Hi. I hear you both like animals."

Mandy and James nodded.

"Have you ever done any riding?" Mrs Hughes asked.

"Not really," Mandy said, "although we have helped friends look after their ponies."

"Can they have a ride on Lady, Mum?" Sara asked.

Mrs Hughes nodded. "How about tomorrow morning? If you'd like to, of course."

"Oh, yes please!" gasped Mandy and James.

"Come round tomorrow about ten, then," said Mrs Hughes. "We'll see how you get on."

"Great," said Mr Hope, "but now it's time for lunch."

They ate lunch sitting outside the caravan. There was cold meat and Gran's home-made vegetarian quiche, together with bowls of potato salad and creamy coleslaw. Mandy and James helped themselves to plates and knives and forks.

Mr Hope offered the cold meat round. "Chicken anyone?" Blackie looked up from his marrow-bone. "Not you, Blackie!" Mr Hope chuckled.

"It's his favourite food," James said. He looked firmly at the young dog. "But you're not having any until we've finished, Blackie."

"You've done us proud, Dorothy," Grandad said to Gran, sitting down in his chair with an overflowing plate.

Mandy sighed happily. "This is what holidays should be like!" she said, as they started to eat.

James finally pushed away his plate and lay back on the grass. "I can't move!" he said.

"You've got to!" said Mandy, putting down her plate and jumping to her feet. "It's time to go and meet Sara."

"Mandy," said Mr Hope, raising his dark eyebrows, "what about the washing-up?"

Mandy's face fell.

Gran smiled at her. "Go on, I'll let you off. You go and see those ponies."

Mandy looked at her dad. He nodded. "Thanks, Gran!" Mandy said. She grabbed her sweatshirt. "Come *on*, James!"

"Can we take Blackie?" James asked, getting to his feet and looking at Blackie, who was still chewing on his bone.

"I would have thought so," said Mrs Hope. "But take a strong lead with you in case you need to tie him up."

Mandy, James and Blackie set off for the cottage. They found Sara filling up a water bucket by the stables. "Hi!" she said, turning off the tap.

"This is Blackie," James said. "I hope you don't mind me bringing him."

Sara shook her head and patted Blackie. "I love dogs!" she said, giggling as Blackie licked her face and hands, his whole body wagging from side to side. Lady put her head out of one of the stables and kicked the door.

"I think she wants to go out into the paddock," said Sara. "I thought I'd better keep her and Mischief in their stables while I had lunch, in case Mischief tried to escape again." She took down Lady and Mischief's head-collars and lead-ropes from a hook by the stable door. "Will you help me put them back out in the field?"

They led the ponies down to the field. As soon as Mischief was released, he cantered round the paddock, his head held high, his tail up. He looked so sweet and small it was difficult to imagine him being naughty, until he stopped and snorted in the middle of the field, his brown mane sticking up like a brush.

"Let's go and hide now and see what Mischief does," Sara said.

Mandy looked round. "Where?"

"How about behind those bushes?" suggested James, pointing to a clump of trees and bushes a little way off from the field.

"Good idea," agreed Sara. They ran with Blackie to the trees and hid in the shadows.

At first, Mischief rolled. Then he started to graze.

It was cool in the shadow of the trees and Mandy shivered slightly. "What if Mischief doesn't try to escape?" she asked.

"I'm sure he will," said Sara.

She was right. After about five minutes, Mischief seemed to get bored with grazing. He trotted to the fence, gazed at the golf course, looked at the wire then, turning, hurried across the field towards the little gate which led to the muckheap.

He stopped by the gate and put his nose near the top. "What's he doing?" whispered James.

"Look!" gasped Mandy. "He's pulling the bolt back."

The little foal carefully pulled back the metal bolt with his teeth. The gate swung open. "He can't get out that way," Sara said. "There's a fence all the way round the muckheap."

The muckheap was a hill of dirty straw about two metres high. Mischief started to climb up it, his back legs pushing him forward in a series of little jumps. He reached the top and looked round.

Mandy laughed. The little foal looked really funny just standing there on top of the muckheap.

"*Now* what's he going to do?" asked James.

"Come back into the field?" suggested Sara. But Mischief had no intention of coming back into the field. He carefully stepped down the far side of the muckheap, stopped halfway down, then jumped over the fence and landed on the grass beyond.

Mandy, James and Sara watched, speechless, as Mischief shook his head and trotted quickly across the campsite in the direction of the golf course.

"Quick," gasped Sara, jumping to her feet. "After him!"

5

Mandy's good idea

Mandy, James and Sara raced across the campsite after Mischief. The little foal disappeared into the trees that separated the campsite and the golf course.

"I hope Mr Benson isn't there!" panted Mandy.

James was being pulled along by Blackie.

He entered the trees just ahead of the others. "I can see him!" he called.

"Who? Mr Benson?" cried Mandy in alarm.

"No. Mischief!" gasped James.

"Don't run up behind him," said Sara frantically, "or he'll run away!"

James struggled to stop Blackie. "Hang on, Blackie. Whoa!"

He managed to stop the puppy just in time. Mischief was standing on the edge of the golf course. He turned his head back to look at them, his tiny brown ears pricked. Sara reached into her pocket. "Here, boy," she murmured, rustling her packet of mints.

Mischief looked at the golf course again.

"Come on, Mischief. Mints . . ." said Sara, edging towards him.

Hearing the rustle of the sweet papers, Mischief looked back. Sara stood still and held her hand out. The foal was too greedy: he came trotting back along the path. Craning his neck, he grabbed the sweet

and tried to set off again but Sara was too quick. She grabbed his mane and hung on to him. After a few steps, Mischief stopped.

"Thank goodness!" said Mandy, sighing with relief.

Sara led Mischief back down the path towards Mandy and James. "You're a naughty boy," she scolded him. "You mustn't try and escape."

Mischief looked at her. *Who, me?* he seemed to say.

They took him back to the paddock,

where Lady was still grazing peacefully. "At least we now know *how* he's escaping," said James, as they opened the main gate and let him go.

Sara nodded. "I'll ask Dad to put a bottom kick bolt on the muckheap gate tonight." She shook her head. "It doesn't seem to matter what we do: he always finds a new way out. He seems to think it's a game."

Mandy looked at Mischief as he wandered round the paddock. If Mr Benson found him on the golf course again, it was a game that could have a very unhappy ending for the little foal. "We need to stop him *wanting* to get out," she said.

"I know," said Sara, her cheerful face looking worried. "But how?"

Later that afternoon, James and Mandy took Blackie for a walk on the beach. As the dog bounded back and forth, they talked about how they could help Sara and

Mischief. But what could they do to make Mischief want to stay in his field? It seemed a very difficult problem to solve.

"Can you think of anything?" Mandy asked her mum and dad, as they all sat round a campfire that evening.

Mr and Mrs Hope shook their heads. "It's very hard," said Mrs Hope, cradling a cup of coffee in her hands. "Mischief sounds like he's a very clever little foal who's determined to escape."

Mandy nodded. She stroked Blackie, who was lying between her and James, chewing on the remains of his marrow-bone.

"That bone certainly seems to have kept Blackie quiet," Gran said.

Grandad chuckled. "It's a pity foals don't like bones," he said. "Dogs are a lot easier to keep amused."

Mandy stared. "Grandad! That's it!" she exclaimed, sitting up. She looked around at the others. "Of course!"

"Of course what?" asked James, looking confused.

"If we keep Mischief amused, he won't try to find ways to escape."

Mrs Hope frowned. "How will you do that?"

"We could put all sorts of things in his field for him to play with," said Mandy. "We could have containers with food hidden in them – or we could put down trails of food and things like that."

"A foal playground!" exclaimed James.

"It's actually not a bad idea," said Mrs Hope, looking interested. "If you keep him busy, he's much less likely to *want* to escape."

"A foal playground," said Grandad shaking his head. "Whatever next?"

"We can plan it out with Sara tomorrow," James said to Mandy.

Mandy leaned back beside Blackie, her mind racing over all the things they could do to keep Mischief out of trouble. She stroked Blackie's ears. Was her idea going to work?

★　★　★

"A playground for Mischief!" Sara said the next morning. "It's a brilliant idea! Come on – let's make a list of all the things we can put in it."

They followed her through to the cottage kitchen. "I thought we could hide food in containers somehow," said Mandy, "and get him to find it."

"We could use buckets," said Sara, getting some paper to make a list with. "We could put them upside down, with the treats underneath. And we can find him a ball to play with. Mum used to have a pony who loved playing with a football."

"What about putting food under some of the cones as well?" suggested James. He had noticed some orange and white cones in the ponies' field the day before.

"OK," said Sara, writing it down.

Just then, Fiona Hughes came into the kitchen. "Hello!" she said, her dark eyes smiling. "What are you three up to?"

Sara explained and showed her mum the list. "The football is a great idea," she said.

"But it won't take him very long to turn the buckets and cones over and get the food out. Maybe you should think of something that would take him a little bit longer to get into."

James eyes widened suddenly. "I know!" he said. "Blackie's got this plastic ball to stop him chewing everything. It's got a hole in it. You put treats inside so that when he rolls the ball around the treats fall out, one at a time. It stops him getting bored. We could make something like that for Mischief."

"That would be perfect," agreed Mrs Hughes, running a hand through her short dark hair. "But you want something he can't crack if he kicks at it."

"We could use a bucket and make a lid for it," said Sara. "He could kick a bucket around as much as he liked. We could call it . . ." She thought for a moment. "The Foal Feeder!" she said, pleased with the name.

Her mother smiled. "I think that's an

excellent idea." She looked at Mandy and James. "Now, do you two still want to have a ride on Lady this morning?"

"Yes please!" they said.

"Well, why don't you get her in from the field and groom her, then?" Mrs Hughes said.

Mandy, James and Sara went out to the field and brought Lady in.

"You start with a dandy-brush, don't you?" Mandy asked, picking up a brush with stiff, dark bristles from Sara's grooming kit. Back in Welford, one of their school friends, Paul Stevens, had a pony called Paddy. She and James often helped Paul with grooming him.

Mrs Hughes nodded. "It gets rid of all the mud and grass stains." She picked out a softer brush. "James, you can use this on Lady's tail."

"And I'll pick her feet out," said Sara.

"Won't Mischief mind us riding Lady?" James asked, as they fetched the saddle and bridle. "She *is* his mother."

"He might whinny a bit," Mrs Hughes replied. "But he was weaned last month. Lady went to stay at a friend's stable so he could get used to being on his own and not suckling from her any more."

Luckily Sara's riding-hat was the right size for both Mandy and James. "Excellent!" said Mrs Hughes, taking Lady's reins and leading her down to the field. "Now, let's get you on. Who's going first? Mandy?"

Mandy nodded eagerly. Sara and James leaned on the gate and watched. In no time at all, Mrs Hughes had Mandy up in the saddle on Lady's back and was showing her how to hold the reins.

"That's fine," said Mrs Hughes, standing back and looking at her. "Now, heels down and head up." She took hold of Lady's bridle. "And walk on, Lady."

Lady set off steadily. Mandy tried to do everything Mrs Hughes said. She grinned at James and Sara as she went past.

"We'll try a trot," Mrs Hughes said, after

a bit. "Hold on tightly to the front of the saddle, and try and move up and down when I say."

Soon they were trotting round with Mrs Hughes calling out, "Up, down; up, down . . ."

When they finally stopped, Mandy was rather breathless and very hot. It felt more as though she was being bounced around, rather than going up and down when she wanted to.

"It gets easier with practice!" said Mrs Hughes, laughing as she saw Mandy's face. She looked at James. "Your turn now, James."

Mandy stood with Sara as Mrs Hughes went through exactly the same thing with James. When they stopped, his face was red and hot, but he was smiling. "That was great!" he said.

Mrs Hughes looked at them kindly. "You both did very well. I think you're going to be natural riders. I'll give you another go this afternoon if you like." She looked thoughtful. "If you practise each day, you might be good enough to go on a picnic ride by the end of the week. We could borrow a pony from the riding-school for Sara to ride, and you two could take it in turns to ride Lady. If the weather stays like this, it could be rather fun."

Sara nodded eagerly. "It's a brilliant idea, Mum." She turned to Mandy and James. "Picnic rides are great!"

Mrs Hughes looked at them. "You'll have to practise hard though, if you're are going to be good enough. Do you want to give it a go?"

Mandy and James looked at each other. "Oh, yes!" they exclaimed.

6

The foal playground

After lunch, Mandy, James and Sara started to organise Mischief's playground. "We can see what we can find in Dad's shed," Sara said. "It's full of junk."

They followed her to a large wooden shed behind the stables. "Dad hates throwing things away so he puts everything in here," Sara told Mandy and James as she opened the door. "I'm sure there are some old buckets and there'll be other things we can use as well."

The shed was crammed with old, dusty objects — gardening tools, furniture, broken toys, boxes of books. Mandy had never seen so much junk. Sara started to root around. "Here's an old football!" she said. "Mischief can play with that."

"And what about this?" James suggested, pulling back a piece of canvas to reveal an old car tyre. "We could tie it to a tree. Mischief could push it with his nose. And there are some more plastic cones," he said pointing to the back.

Mandy spotted a pile of old buckets in a corner. She clambered over a faded armchair and three boxes of magazines to get to them. "These will be perfect to put treats in," she said, picking up two of them. She dumped them by the door.

Sara looked at the pile of stuff. "Come

on! That's enough. Let's start putting things out."

They washed everything under the stable tap, scrubbing each article with an old brush until all the dust and grime had come off. Blackie lay down and watched them from a shady spot by the stables.

Mandy picked one of the buckets up and examined it. "We've got to put holes in it somehow and then cover the top," she said.

Sara frowned. "I think we'd better ask Dad how to make the holes. We'll never cut through the plastic with scissors. Maybe he'll know how best to cover the top too."

Alex Hughes readily agreed to help them. "Anything to keep that foal out of trouble!" he said, chuckling. They showed him the buckets and explained about the Foal Feeder. "Let me see what I can do," he said, taking the buckets away. Meanwhile, Mandy, James and Sara carried everything else over to the field. They put out the football, tied the tyre to the branch of the oak-tree in one corner of the field, and set up the cones in the middle of the field with an apple underneath each one. Mischief soon realised what they were doing and, as fast as they put out the cones, he knocked them over and ate the apples.

Just then, Alex Hughes returned with the buckets. He had drilled holes in the sides for the treats to fall out of. He had also found a way to fasten the two buckets together with metal clips, making one large oval container that was easy to open and shut.

"It's brilliant!" said James, examining it.

Sara unfastened the clips and put a few handfuls of pony nuts into the buckets. "Let's see if it works," she said, clipping the buckets together and rolling them along the ground. The pony nuts rattled around inside and a few fell out.

"Very clever!" said Alex Hughes.

Hearing the rattle of the bucket, Mischief came over to investigate. Sara rolled the Foal Feeder towards him and a few more pony nuts fell out. Mischief gobbled them

up and looked hard at the bucket. He nudged it with his nose and it rolled a little way. Mischief eagerly ate the pony nuts that fell out. He pushed again at the bucket – harder this time.

Mandy grinned. "I think he likes it!" She looked round the field. "There are so many things for him to play with. Surely he won't want to escape now."

Sara looked at the little foal and held up her crossed fingers. "I hope not," she said.

★ ★ ★

By the time Mandy and James got back to the caravan, they had watched Mischief play with everything in his playground, ridden Lady one more time, groomed Mischief *and* helped clean up the stable yard. Their jeans were thick with dust and dirt and their hair was sticking up all over the place. Mrs Hope took one look at them and suggested that it might be the ideal time for a swim in the sea.

"Oh yes!" said Mandy eagerly.

They shrugged off their dirty clothes and pulled on their swimsuits. "Where are Gran and Grandad?" Mandy asked, as they joined Mr and Mrs Hope at the top of the cliff path.

"Out golfing," Mrs Hope replied, as they set off down to the beach with Blackie bouncing beside them.

Their flip-flops sank into the soft sand, the warm grains tickling their toes. "Race you to the sea!" James called to Mandy.

Mandy charged after him to the water's edge. Blackie bounced straight past them, drenching them both. They squealed as the cold water hit their skin. "It's cold!" Mandy gasped, taking a step back.

"Chicken!" Mr Hope teased Mandy from a safe distance. Blackie stopped bouncing in the water and his ears pricked up.

Mandy's hand flew to her mouth. "I don't think you should have said that, Dad!" she said, as Blackie shot out of the water and raced over to where Mr Hope was standing. Looking up eagerly, Blackie shook himself hard. Water sprayed all over Mr Hope.

"Blackie!" gasped James.

Mrs Hope burst out laughing.

"What the . . ." spluttered Mr Hope.

Mandy giggled. "Well, you did say 'chicken', Dad. Blackie thought you were going to give him some!"

"Well," said Mr Hope, looking at Mandy and James giggling by the water's edge, "you two look far too dry to me!" He ran across the sand towards them. Squealing, they dashed into the sea.

★ ★ ★

When Gran and Grandad got back from playing golf, they found Mandy and James helping to get supper ready.

"How was the golf?" Mrs Hope asked them.

"Excellent," Grandad replied, sitting down at the table and helping himself to a piece of tomato Mandy had just chopped up. "The clubhouse was buzzing with news. Richard Frost is coming to play at the golf course later this week."

Mandy and James stopped chopping up tomatoes and looked puzzled.

"Richard Frost is a famous golfer," Mr Hope explained to them. "He also happens to be the captain of the golf club here." He grinned. "I should think they'll be trying to make sure the place looks perfect for his visit."

Mandy thought about the bad-tempered green-keeper. "Then Mr Benson will be so busy, he won't have time to worry about Mischief," she said hopefully, putting the tomatoes in the salad bowl and picking up the cucumber.

"How *is* Mischief?" asked Gran, sitting down. "And what was your day like?"

Mandy and James started to tell her. "Mrs Hughes said we might be able to go on a picnic ride on Friday if our riding's good enough," Mandy said.

"But we've got to learn how to do the rising trot by then," James added, putting out the knives and forks. He frowned. "It's very bouncy."

"Mrs Hughes is going to give us another lesson in the morning," Mandy said.

"That's very kind of her," said Mrs Hope, who was peeling potatoes. "I hope you two have been helpful and not got in the way."

Mandy nodded. "We groomed Lady and Mischief."

"And helped brush the yard," said James.

"And we've made the playground for Mischief, so we hope he won't try to escape any more," said Mandy.

"It certainly sounds like you've been busy." Gran smiled.

"We have," said Mandy, with a grin. "But it was so much fun!"

The next morning they got to the stables to find Sara mucking out Lady's stable. "Hi!" she said, as they looked over the door. She wiped a hand across her hot face. "I thought I'd get this done early. I only have to do it once a week at the moment because Lady and Mischief spend most of their time in the field. Thank goodness!"

"Can we help?" Mandy asked eagerly.

"If you want," said Sara, looking surprised. James tied Blackie up outside, and soon he and Mandy were hard at work. James filled Lady's water bucket up while Mandy and Sara fetched some clean straw from the barn. James staggered back with the bucket, spilling half of it down his legs.

"I don't mind!" He grinned. "It keeps me cool."

"Just the wheelbarrow to empty now,"

said Mandy. She picked up the handles of the full wheelbarrow and pushed it carefully towards the field.

"I'll do the gate," James offered. He untied Blackie. "Come on then, Blackie." As they wheeled the wheelbarrow to the muckheap and shook out every last bit of dirty straw, Blackie trotted happily around the paddock, investigating all the interesting smells.

"Look at Mischief," Mandy said, as they came back through the field. The little foal was staring over the fence towards the golf course. "I hope he's not planning to escape again," she said, feeling worried.

Sara was waiting for them at the gate. "I set up everything in his playground before I turned him out in the field," she told them. "The trouble is, he's so clever he finds all the treats really quickly. The Foal Feeder kept him interested for a while, but he's already emptied that as well."

James picked up a stick and threw it for Blackie. "We need to think of more things to keep him occupied," he said.

"Like what?" Sara asked.

They puzzled over the question as they threw more sticks for Blackie. He raced after each one, bounding back with it between his teeth. "At least it tires him out," James grinned as Blackie dropped a stick at his feet and stood there, panting.

"It's a pity we can't tire Mischief out so easily." Sara sighed.

Mandy noticed that Mischief was watching them. "Mischief!" she called. The little foal walked over, looking curious.

Blackie picked up a stick and placed it by James's foot. James threw it into the air. "Fetch!" he said, and Blackie raced off.

Mischief put his nose down on the ground, picked up one of Blackie's other sticks and held it in his mouth.

Mandy laughed. "He wants to 'fetch' like Blackie does!"

"He's always picking things up and carrying them around," Sara told her. "Sticks, grooming brushes, buckets."

"Golf balls!" added Mandy, with a grin.

The foal watched as James threw another stick for Blackie. He dropped his stick at Mandy's feet. Mandy laughed. "Go on then, Mischief," she said, picking up the stick and throwing it. "Fetch!"

To Mandy's amazement, Mischief turned and trotted to the stick. He stopped, picked it up in his teeth, looked at them and then carefully carried it back over.

"He *is* fetching it!" Mandy exclaimed.

James looked as if he couldn't believe his eyes. "Horses don't normally fetch, do they?" he asked Sara.

Sara shook her head. "Not normally." She looked at the little foal, who had now dropped the stick at their feet. "But I guess Mischief is a special foal." She praised him and fed him a mint. "Clever boy, Mischief."

"Let's see if he'll do it again," said Mandy. She picked up the stick and threw it. Mischief trotted away and brought it back. "Good boy!" Mandy cried, feeding him some of the pony nuts she had in her pocket. She turned to the others, her eyes shining with an idea. "We could teach him to fetch all sorts of different things – grooming brushes, cones, buckets. It would help to keep him busy."

"That's a brilliant idea!" said James. "He's so clever. If we give him a treat every time he fetches something, he'll probably learn really quickly."

Sara went off to fetch some more pony

nuts. When she came back, they started encouraging Mischief to fetch different things, giving him a reward every time he picked something up and brought it back to them.

Fiona Hughes came down to the gate to find out what they were doing. Sara explained. Mrs Hughes thought it was a very good idea. "But don't overdo the lessons," she warned. "Keep them short; otherwise he might get bored."

"We'll stop now," said Sara. "But we'll do some more later this afternoon."

"In that case," Fiona said, "you can bring Lady in and groom her ready for Mandy and James's riding lesson." She looked at Mandy and James. "Let's see if we can get you doing a rising trot today."

Mandy and James didn't manage the rising trot that morning, but they kept practising hard. Over the next few days, they spent every minute they could helping Sara with Mischief and Lady. The weather stayed hot, so they tried to train Mischief and ride either first thing in the morning or later in the afternoon. The rest of the time they spent grooming, mucking out, brushing up the stable yard, and cleaning the tack. Sometimes they just sat in the field under the oak-tree, watching Mischief and Lady graze. When it got too hot, they walked down to the beach to cool off in the sea.

On Thursday they lay in the shade of the oak-tree drinking cans of lemonade. Mischief was grazing round their feet, his teeth tearing at the short grass.

"This is a brilliant holiday!" James said.

"The best!" Mandy agreed. She picked up a couple of fallen branches and threw them a little way across the ground. "Fetch!" she said. Blackie jumped up eagerly and bounded out to get one of the sticks, while Mischief trotted to the other. Mandy grinned. Mischief was getting really very good at fetching. "Good boy," she said, feeding him some pony nuts from her pocket. He nudged her, but she pushed him away. "No. No more," she said.

Mischief wandered over to the fence. He looked at the wire between the two bars, then tried to poke his head through. "No, Mischief!" Mandy shouted. The foal backed off.

Sara looked worried. "He still wants to get out."

Mandy nodded. It was true. Several times in the last few days she had noticed Mischief inspecting the fence or sticking his head through the wire. The trouble was, he got bored so easily. As long as he was getting attention from them or had fresh treats in his toys, he was happy, but as soon as he was left on his own, he started looking longingly towards the golf course and freedom.

James was looking at Sara's anxious face. "He won't get out. The field's really secure now," he said.

Mandy nodded. "After all, he hasn't escaped since the day we met you," she added.

Sara looked at them, then gave a half-smile. "You're right," she said. "It *is* silly to worry. Mischief hasn't got out in the last few days." Her eyes lit up. "Anyway, we've got the picnic ride to think about."

"Do you think your mum is going to let us go?" James asked. "She didn't mention it yesterday or today."

Sara got to her feet. "Come on. Let's find out."

Fiona Hughes wanted to see Mandy and James ride one more time before she decided about the picnic ride. For the first time, they both managed to do a rising trot during the lesson.

"Well done!" Mrs Hughes called out, as Mandy trotted Lady round the paddock all by herself. She had found the rhythm of the trot now and could make herself go up and down to fit in with Lady's stride.

"It makes trotting much less bouncy!" Mandy said, slowing Lady back to a walk. She patted the grey pony's neck.

"Well," Sara demanded, "can we go on the picnic ride, Mum?"

They held their breath. What would Mrs Hughes say? She looked at them, then her dark eyes lit up as she smiled. "I don't see why not," she said.

"Oh, Mum, thank you!" cried Sara. She looked at Mandy and James in excitement. "We've got so much to plan."

As they untacked Lady and put her back in the paddock, they discussed where they would go and what they would take.

"There are some maps inside," said Sara. She got out three cans of cola and they sat round the table looking at a map. They planned out a route that would take them along the beach, down some bridle-paths and through a wood before ending up back at the campsite.

"There's a big field where we can eat our picnic," Sara said. "And tables and places to tie up the ponies." Mrs Hughes had rung up her friend at the local riding-school and arranged for Sara to borrow a pony for the day. Mandy and James would take it in turns to ride Lady. The person who wasn't riding was going to use Sara's mountain bike.

"We can carry the picnic in our rucksacks," said Sara.

"I bet Gran will let us have some cakes," said Mandy.

"And biscuits," added James. He loved Mandy's gran's cooking.

When everything had been planned out,

they went to clean Lady's tack. "Should we go and check on Mischief?" Mandy suggested. "He's been on his own for quite a bit."

Sara shook her head. "Like you said, there's no point worrying. He can't get out of the field any more." She headed for the tack room. "Let's get the saddle soap and the tack."

They sat outside the stables in the sun, carefully removing the dirt and grease from the saddle and bridle using warm water. They rubbed saddle soap into the leather until it gleamed.

"There, that looks much better!" said James, examining the finished bridle from all angles. He threw his sponge into the water bucket. It splashed water all over Sara, who was kneeling on the ground finishing off the stirrup leathers.

"*James!*" she exclaimed, throwing her sponge at him. It bounced off his shoulder.

James looked round, saw another sponge on the floor and threw it. It sailed straight past Sara and hit Mandy on the head.

"Hey!" said Mandy, and flung her sponge at James. Soon there were more wet sponges flying through the air.

When James got hit on the nose by a particularly soggy sponge, he picked up the water bucket. "Right!" he cried.

"No!" Sara and Mandy gasped, laughing and running away towards the house.

Clip-clop! Clip-clop! They stopped suddenly as they heard the sound of quick, light hooves coming down the path at the side of the house.

"Who's that?" Sara asked Mandy.

"Is anybody there?" came an angry shout. Mr Benson was marching round the side of the house. His face was red with anger, and in one hand he held a rope. Mandy, Sara and James gasped.

At the end of the rope was Mischief!

7

One last chance

"Mr Benson!" said Sara in dismay.

Mr Benson marched up to her. He looked furious! "This animal was on the golf course again," he shouted. "It's left hoofprints all over my greens!"

"I'm really, *really* sorry," said Sara, sounding upset.

"Sorry isn't going to help!" exclaimed Mr Benson. He was only a small man, but the rage that filled him seemed to make him three times bigger. "The captain's coming to play tomorrow. What's he going to say?" He didn't wait for an answer. "I've given you fair warning, young lady, but this time enough's enough. I'm ringing the council!"

"No!" cried Sara desperately.

Mandy stepped forward, her concern for Mischief overcoming her fear of Mr Benson. "Please don't, Mr Benson," she begged.

Mr Benson frowned. "Who are you?"

"I'm Mandy Hope. I'm on holiday here."

Mr Benson's eyes narrowed. "Haven't I seen you on the golf course?"

Mandy nodded. "With my mum and dad, and my grandparents." Her eyes pleaded with the angry man. "If Mischief has to be tethered, he might hurt himself. He might break a leg. Please don't tell the council."

The anger in Mr Benson's eyes seemed to fade slightly. "I don't want him to get injured," he said, in a more reasonable tone of voice. "But what else can I do? I can't have him on the golf course." He ran a hand through his thin hair. "If I don't keep it in tip-top condition, I lose my job, you see."

"We'll make sure he doesn't ever escape again, won't we?" Mandy said, turning to James and Sara. They both nodded quickly.

"Please give him one more chance, Mr Benson," pleaded Sara.

Mr Benson considered for a moment. "All right," he said at last. "But this is it. One last chance. If I find him on the course once more, I'm telling the council." Shaking his head, he turned and marched away.

Mischief watched him go. Then he put his head down to graze on the tufts of grass sticking up on the path.

"Oh, Mischief!" said Mandy, putting her arm round the foal's neck.

"What am I going to do?" asked Sara.

"Don't worry," Mandy said. "We'll help you think of something."

"But we've tried *everything*!" said Sara.

Mischief wandered to the gate and whinnied to Lady. "Should I let him in?" said James.

Sara nodded. James put Mischief in the field, then they slowly started to clear up the yard. They didn't speak. Mandy picked up a sponge and some saddle soap. Ten minutes ago, they had been having so much fun, but now not one of them felt like smiling.

"How could he have got out?" Sara asked in despair, as they put the tack away.

"I don't know," said James, shaking his head. "We'll have to find out."

They went down to the paddock. Lady was grazing by the cones. "Where's Mischief?" asked Mandy.

"Oh no," whispered Sara, her face going white as she looked round the empty field. "He can't have gone again already."

They ran into the field. "Look! Over there," cried James pointing to the oak-tree. Mischief was standing by the fence behind the tree. With one front hoof, he was holding down the wire that ran between the top and bottom rails of the fence. He was squeezing his body through the tiny gap.

"He's getting *between* the two wires!" Mandy exclaimed.

"No!" cried Sara, racing towards him.

Mischief turned and looked. Alarmed at being caught, he backed hastily out of the hole and cantered off towards Lady, his head and tail held high.

"So that's how he got out," said Mandy.

Sara shook her head. "It's impossible. He's too clever – we're never going to be able to stop him escaping."

"Can't your dad put a second wire in place?" suggested James.

"He's bound to get through that, as well," Sara replied.

"What about putting up a different

type of fence?" Mandy asked.

"Mum and Dad can't possibly afford it at the moment," Sara said. "Not with all the costs of getting the campsite up and running this year." She shook her head. "I can't leave him out here. We'd better bring him in."

Reluctantly, they put Mischief in his stable. He wandered around for a bit sniffing the straw, then came and looked at them expectantly. *All right,* he seemed to say. *I've checked out the stable, now I want to go back outside, please.*

"You can't go out," Sara said sadly, looking at him. "You'll just escape again."

Fiona Hughes came out from the house. "What are the long faces for?" she said in surprise, seeing them standing round the stable.

Sara explained.

Mrs Hughes' face grew serious. "Oh dear," she said.

"What are we going to do, Mum?" Sara asked.

"I guess we'll just have to keep him in his stable," Mrs Hughes said. "Perhaps when he's a bit older, he'll be less mischievous."

"You mean, not let him out in the field at all?" said Sara.

"Not until we've thought of a foolproof way to stop him escaping," said her mother.

"But he'll hate being in his stable all the time!" Sara exclaimed.

"But if he gets out of the field one

more time, we'll be forced to keep him tethered," Mrs Hughes said. "Sorry love, but there's nothing else we can do." She sighed sadly. "Look, why don't you go and fill a hay-net for him? That will keep him happy for a bit."

Mandy and James followed Sara up to the barn.

"He's going to hate being in his stable," Sara said. "He'll get so bored."

When they came back to the stable, Mischief tried to push past them as soon as they opened the door. "No, get back!" Sara said, going in with the hay-net.

Mischief's dark eyes looked puzzled. He obviously didn't understand why he had to be in the stable when he could be out in the sunshine with his mother. He looked hopefully at Mandy and James as they leaned over the door. But when they didn't open it, he stepped back sadly into the middle of the stable. His head dropped and he ignored the hay-net.

"Don't worry, Mischief," Mandy said

softly. "We'll think of something." She met Sara and James's doubtful eyes. "I *promise* we will!" she said.

8

Fetch!

Mandy and James lay in their sleeping bags, both of them staring at the tent roof. They had one thing on their minds – Mischief.

"I hope he's not too unhappy shut up in his stable," said Mandy, trying to get comfortable. All week she had been falling asleep as soon as she got into her sleeping bag, but tonight the ground seemed uncomfortable.

"If only we could think of a way to help," James said through the darkness. "But even your mum and dad didn't have any ideas."

Mandy sighed. Mr and Mrs Hope had listened sympathetically to the problem, but, like Fiona Hughes had said, the only option seemed to be to keep Mischief in his stable for the moment.

There was silence for a while, then James spoke. "We've got the picnic ride tomorrow."

"I know," Mandy said flatly. They had been so excited about it earlier, but now it didn't seem so much fun. How could they go and enjoy themselves while Mischief was miserable?

"I wish we weren't going home on Saturday. It'll be really hard leaving, knowing that Mischief and Sara are unhappy," said James.

Mandy tried to look on the bright side.

"At least Mr Benson didn't get in touch with the council. We've still got one last chance to think of something."

"One last chance and one last day," said James.

Mandy's mind raced. What could they do?

Sara was mucking out Mischief's stable when they arrived the next morning. She looked pale and her eyes were red.

"How's Mischief?" James asked.

Sara sighed. "He wouldn't eat his feed this morning and he didn't touch the hay-net last night."

"But he's normally so greedy," said Mandy.

Sara nodded. "He just hates being shut in the stable. He looks really miserable."

Mandy tried to make Sara see the bright side. "It could be worse. If Mr Benson had reported Mischief, he would have to be tethered or stay in his stable all the time. At least we've still got a chance to think of something."

"That's true," said Sara, cheering up slightly.

"Where *is* Mischief?" asked James, looking into the other two stables.

Sara looked as if she thought James had gone mad. "Tied up by the gate, of course."

Mandy and James looked at the gate. There was a piece of string hanging from it, but no sign of Mischief. Mandy's heart leaped into her mouth. "He's not there," she whispered.

Sara dashed out of the stable and stared

at the gate. "Oh no! He must have escaped." She ran to the gate, panic on her face. "I tied him up here about five minutes ago. I didn't want to put him in the field in case he got out again. He must have managed to undo his rope!"

"We've got to find him!" Mandy gasped.

"I bet he's on the golf course," Sara said, in dismay.

Mandy's heart raced. "Come on!"

"The captain of the golf course is there today," panted James as they ran across the campsite. "I heard Mandy's gran talking about it. So Mr Benson will be there and Mischief's bound to be caught."

"Don't say that," cried Mandy. If Mr Benson found Mischief again, then it really would be the end for him – especially if important Mr Frost heard about the naughty foal.

They ran through the trees and onto the golf course. There was no sign of Mischief. "Where is he?" asked Mandy, looking round. She could see two golfers in the distance. One of the men, wearing a bright-red and blue checked jumper, was just lifting his golf club to hit the ball. But there was no brown-and-white foal.

"Maybe he *didn't* come over here," said Sara, her eyes lighting up with hope. "Perhaps he stayed on the campsite looking for food."

"There's Mr Benson!" said James. The green-keeper was standing at the edge of one of the greens watching the two golfers. The man in the red and blue jumper hit the ball. It flew off course, bouncing and landing in the rough not too far away from where Mandy, James and Sara were standing.

"Mr Benson's spotted us!" said Sara, seeing the green-keeper looking at them. "Quick, let's go! Mischief obviously isn't here."

Sara and James made their way towards the trees, but Mandy took one last look round. Still no Mischief. She was just turning to follow the others when the golfer who had lost his ball came over and called out to her. "You didn't happen to see a golf ball land in the grass round here, did you?"

Mandy pointed to where she had seen the ball fall. "It's over there," she said.

The golfer smiled, his eyes crinkling up at the corners in a friendly way. "Thanks," he said. "It can be really difficult to find lost balls in grass like this." He waved his friend over.

"Mandy, come on!" James and Sara urged from the trees.

Mandy suddenly realised that Mr Benson was striding towards her. She turned to run.

"What the . . ." A loud exclamation stopped Mandy in her tracks. She looked back to see the golfer and his companion standing with their mouths wide open as Mischief came trotting swiftly out of a clump of trees a little further up the course.

"Oh no!" Mandy gasped, spinning round

and catching a look of surprise and fury on Mr Benson's face.

She started to run towards the little foal, but Mischief was too far ahead of her. He trotted towards the patch of rough grass where the golfer's ball had landed. Then he stopped and picked it up in his mouth.

"Well I never!" gasped the golfer.

Mandy could see the little foal was about to trot back to the cover of the trees. "Mischief!" she called suddenly. The little foal stopped and looked round. "Mischief, fetch!"

Mischief hesitated for a moment. Mandy rustled a sweet paper in her pocket. Pricking up his ears, Mischief trotted straight over to her. He stopped in front of her and dropped the golf ball gently into her outstretched hand.

"Good boy!" cried Mandy, feeding him a couple of mints. James and Sara forgot all about Mr Benson in their delight and ran over. "Wasn't he brilliant?" Mandy said to them.

"That's amazing!" said the golfer, hurrying over.

Mandy handed back the golf ball. "Sorry," she apologised, "but he hasn't chewed it or anything."

"Don't be sorry," said the golfer, stroking Mischief enthusiastically. "I've never seen anything like it! Who does he belong to?"

"Sara," Mandy replied, introducing her friend.

"My parents own the campsite next door," Sara explained. "He's called Mischief."

Mischief pushed against the man in a friendly manner. The golfer laughed. "He's enchanting!" he exclaimed.

"Hey!" Mr Benson shouted, coming over to them.

Mandy turned. "Oh no," she said, her heart sinking.

"What's the matter?" asked the golfer.

"Mr Benson," said Mandy, gulping as she saw the green-keeper marching over, his face clouded with anger. She looked at the man desperately. "He said if Mischief got on to the golf course one more time, then he was going to tell the council. They'll make Sara tether Mischief or keep him in his stable all the time." Hot tears sprang to her eyes as she blurted out the whole story. "If he has to be tethered, he might hurt himself. And if he's in his stable all day, he'll be miserable."

The golfer looked concerned. "We can't let that happen!" he said.

"Tell that to Mr Benson," muttered

James, as Mr Benson reached them, closely followed by the golfer's friend.

"This is the last straw!" the green-keeper was shouting angrily. "I told you to keep that foal off the golf course. Well, no more warnings! I'm going to the council today." He turned to the golfer, his face suddenly anxious. "I'm so terribly sorry, Mr Frost, sir. I've told these children to keep that foal off the golf course time and time again."

Mandy frowned. Mr Frost? Wasn't that the name of the famous golfer and captain of the club?

Mr Benson came closer, looking flustered. "I'll get something done about it, you'll see, sir."

"I won't hear of it!" Mr Frost said firmly.

Mr Benson looked very surprised. "But—"

The man turned to Mandy, James and Sara. "My name is Richard Frost," he announced. "I am the captain of this golf club and under no circumstances will I allow your enchanting little foal to be punished for his remarkable talent. In my opinion, I see him as an added bonus for the club. Just think how happy the golfers who play on this course will be if they never lose a golf ball again!" He smiled broadly and turned to his friend. "What do you say, Peter?"

His friend nodded. Stepping forwards, he introduced himself to Mandy, James and Sara. "I'm Peter Edwards, the treasurer of the club," he said. He looked at Mischief. "A foal who can find missing golf balls. Well, well. He certainly sounds like a find to me."

Mr Frost turned to the speechless Mr Benson. "Mr Benson," he declared, "the foal stays. He can go where he pleases."

"But . . . but . . . what about my greens?" stammered Mr Benson. "His hoof-marks. The greens won't be fit to play on."

Mr Frost paused for a moment and frowned. Mandy held her breath. Surely he wasn't going to change his mind?

Mr Frost's face suddenly lit up. "I have an idea! The club can pay to install low-voltage electric fences around the greens. I've seen it done on other golf courses in the countryside. How about it, Peter?"

Mr Edwards nodded.

"It's ideal," continued Mr Frost. "The foal will be kept off the greens and he can roam the rest of the course as he pleases."

"Electric fences?" said Sara uncertainly.

"Very low-voltage ones," Mr Frost explained. "They'll give him a tiny shock if he touches them. He'll learn very quickly to keep away from the greens."

"I think it's a brilliant idea!" said James.

They looked at Mr Benson. He nodded. "Well," he said, clearing his throat, "I don't see why it shouldn't work." He looked at Mischief. "As long as he keeps off the greens, it could be rather nice having a pony around the place. You know, I never really wanted him to have to be tied up. I didn't know what else to do, you see."

Sara turned to Mr Frost. "Thank you so much," she said.

"No problem," he replied. "I hear your parents are very understanding about the number of golf balls that come on to your campsite." He smiled. "Maybe you can train Mischief to pick those up and bring them back, as well!"

"I'll try!" said Sara, with a grin.

As they led Mischief back to the stables across the campsite, Mr and Mrs Hope, Gran and Grandad drove past them on their way to the golf course. The Land-rover stopped. "What's happened?" Mrs Hope asked, jumping out. Her green eyes looked concerned. "Has he escaped again?"

Mandy nodded. "But it's all right!" she added. "Everything's worked out for the best."

It didn't take Mandy, Sara and James long to explain about Mr Frost's brilliant solution. The Hopes got back into the Land-rover and followed them to the

Hughes' cottage, so they could tell Mrs Hughes the good news.

"I'll see if your mum's in the house," Mrs Hope said.

Mischief looked very sad when Sara put him in his stable. "It's only for one day," she explained to him softly.

"Mr Frost said that he would get the fences put up by tomorrow," Mandy explained to Gran and Grandad, who were looking over the stable door. "Then Mischief will be able to go wherever he wants!" She scratched Mischief's neck and he nuzzled her arm in return. "Soon you'll be having lots of fun again," she said, giving him a hug.

Mrs Hope came over to the stable. "There doesn't seem to be anyone in," she said to Sara.

Sara looked surprised. "Mum should be here," she said.

Suddenly, there was a clip-clopping of hooves coming round the side of the house and Fiona Hughes appeared leading a small black pony. She looked at the Hopes in surprise.

"It's Pippin from the riding-school!" exclaimed Sara, looking at the black pony.

"The picnic ride!" gasped Mandy. In the excitement of the events on the golf course, they had forgotten all about it.

"Where have you been?" Fiona Hughes asked them. "I had to go and collect Pippin from the riding-school by myself. I thought you were going to come with me."

Mr Hope grinned. "It's a long story, Fiona."

"But it's got a great ending!" added James.

"Oh, Mum. Wait till you hear!" cried Sara.

When Mrs Hughes heard the news, she hugged Sara. "What an excellent idea," she said.

Mr Hope rubbed his hands together. "Now, weren't you all supposed to be going on a picnic ride?"

With everyone helping, it took no time

at all to catch and groom Lady, and put on her tack. James said Mandy could ride first. She ran to say a quick goodbye to Mischief. Then, with everyone watching, she mounted Lady.

"Look after Mischief, Mum," Sara called, gathering up Pippin's reins.

"I will," Fiona promised. "I'll make sure he's happy."

Gran and Grandad waved. Mischief poked his nose just above the stable door. Mr Hope put his arm round Mrs Hope. "Have a good time," they all called.

Sitting up very straight in the saddle, Mandy squeezed Lady on.

The ponies clip-clopped out of the campsite with James cycling alongside and Blackie trotting ahead of them, poking around in the bushes. The sun was shining and a light breeze lifted the ponies' manes.

"I'm glad we met Mr Frost on the golf course today," said James.

"I'm glad Mischief's going to be allowed

to be his usual adventurous self again,"
added Sara.

Mandy patted Lady's soft grey neck and
smiled happily at them. "Everything's
turned out perfectly!" she said.

If you enjoyed this special Animal Ark Pets story, look out for the Christmas special this autumn:

CAT'S CRADLE

Lucy Daniels

Mandy Hope loves animals and knows lots about them too – both her parents are vets! So Mandy's always able to help her friends with their pet problems . . .

One of the teachers at Mandy's school has found a sweet little cat, whom she names Tinker. But Miss Oswald is busy organising the school nativity play, so can't look after a pet. And Welford's animal sanctuary is full. Will Mandy find someone to take Tinker in?

LUCY DANIELS

Animal Ark Pets

0 340 67283 8	Puppy Puzzle	£3.50	❑
0 340 67284 6	Kitten Crowd	£3.50	❑
0 340 67285 4	Rabbit Race	£3.50	❑
0 340 67286 2	Hamster Hotel	£3.50	❑
0 340 68729 0	Mouse Magic	£3.50	❑
0 340 68730 4	Chick Challenge	£3.50	❑
0 340 68731 2	Pony Parade	£3.50	❑
0 340 68732 0	Guinea-pig Gang	£3.50	❑
0 340 71371 2	Gerbil Genius	£3.50	❑
0 340 71372 0	Duckling Diary	£3.50	❑
0 340 71373 9	Lamb Lessons	£3.50	❑
0 340 71374 7	Doggy Dare	£3.50	❑
0 340 73585 6	Donky Derby	£3.50	❑
0 340 73586 4	Hedgehog Home	£3.50	❑
0 340 73587 2	Frog Friends	£3.50	❑
0 340 73588 0	Bunny Bonanza	£3.50	❑
0 340 71375 5	Cat Crazy	£3.50	❑
0 340 73605 4	Pets' Party	£3.50	❑
0 340 73589 9	Ferret Fun	£3.50	❑

All Hodder Children's books are available at your local bookshop, or can be ordered direct from the publisher. Just tick the titles you would like and complete the details below. Prices and availability are subject to change without prior notice.

Please enclose a cheque or postal order made payable to *Bookpoint Ltd*, and send to: Hodder Children's Books, 39 Milton Park, Abingdon, OXON OX14 4TD, UK. Email Address: orders@bookpoint.co.uk

If you would prefer to pay by credit card, our call centre team would be delighted to take your order by telephone. Our direct line *01235 400414* (lines open 9.00 am–6.00 pm Monday to Saturday, 24 hour message answering service). Alternatively you can send a fax on *01235 400454*.

TITLE		FIRST NAME		SURNAME	

ADDRESS	
DAYTIME TEL:	POST CODE

If you would prefer to pay by credit card, please complete:
Please debit my Visa/Access/Diner's Card/American Express (delete as applicable) card no:

Signature .... Expiry Date: ....

If you would NOT like to receive further information on our products please tick the box. ❑